Chapter One

The holomaps take a little tuning to ensure they're on the right frequency. When the cyber corps rearrange the districts updated maps of Howlchester are sent to them so it has to be right. Cled sends out the updated maps when his network comes across a change made by the cyber corps. The districts change often since the corps want people to use their implants paired with their map subscription and every other subscription in the book while they're at it. Holomaps and other old tech are better. They don't track you, they don't force you to constantly send half of your earnings to corps and most importantly they aren't designed to control you. Cled finished up on the holomap he was preparing, made a few checks to ensure it was up to his standards, scanned the room for anything that could light the workshop on fire and give him away again and then left while putting the fresh holomap in his pack.

Four locks were on the door to the workshop, all fashioned by Cled. The cybers would have a hard job getting through them even with their precious implants. The workshop was in a forgotten basement the corps probably didn't even know existed anymore. With their constant mergers, IP transfers and building repurposing the corps often lost track of things. Even new tech couldn't keep up with the business practices of the corps. Cled climbed rough metal stairs to the surface where he emerged in some back alley. No one was around and it was dark.

 Without his own holomap, Cled couldn't navigate Howlchester anymore. He could when he was a kid, but now it was next to impossible. You used to be able to get away with a 2D map, one that showed the streets from above, but you would be a fool to try and use one of those these days. The streets were interwoven and layered now. Maybe if it was just that you could learn the 3D space that the city had become but the districts changed too often for that. Even since the day before, the districts had changed. Cybersoft now owned the street the workshop was on, when Cled had last been on the street the day before it was owned by Quincy. Cled's holomap said Cled would have to avoid the new district borders to get to the exchange spot for this new holomap. Cled didn't pay the subscriptions for navigation between districts. There were too many of them to keep track of unless you got the "all in one package" which covered most of the districts. The "all in one package" would cost half of Cled's earnings even with his illegal old tech business. He'd be a fool to pay that.

The holomap pointed to an abandoned shop as the nearest way to avoid the district border checks. On the Cybersoft side, it was empty. Cled cautiously made his way inside. He couldn't see anyone. As he went through what had been a book shop his feet crunched on broken glass. The books were damp and mouldy, their information lost to the past. Cybers wouldn't care about that. Their neural implants could shove as much information into their conscious as they liked in seconds. Old books had too much nuance for them anyway. The shop must have had two fronts the other side opened onto a different street which the map said was owned by Youverse. That was confirmed by the Youverse guard patrol marching past logos emblazoned on their chests. Cled hid behind a bookshelf. Best for a non-cyber to not be seen. Even normal citizens with implants these days could cause trouble for a non-cyber but corp guards were best avoided at all costs. Covered from head to toe in implants the guards had bought into corp cyber upgrades more than most.

As he waited Cled checked his wrist where a watch would be. Instead of a watch, he was greeted by a tattoo. It read, "Life is better this way." Cled knew it was. Once there had permanently been a holowatch there. A new tech holowatch. They were addictive and eased anxiety in a way, a precursor to implants. Cled wouldn't use new tech again not after the trouble it had caused him, not after the control he lost by using it. It wasn't cybers he hated it was what you lost by becoming one. The new tech that implants were made from highjacked the mind making you a drone for the corps. At least that's how Cled saw it anyway.

The patrol passed by. Cled took his opportunity and darted into an alley across the road. He wove through the streets up and down, left and right following the holomap. He trusted the map entirely, so much of his time had been spent on making it. It would never let him down as long as the maps were up to date. He came across very few people on his way to the exchange spot. During the daytime, the pedestrian routes in Howlchester were quiet so at night they were practically silent. When the cybers got addicted to their new tech it was all they wanted to do and you could do that from anywhere once you had the implants. There was no need to leave the house other than for work and keep your subscriptions paid.

As always, Cled was early. He couldn't risk being caught. They'd lock him up for years which he couldn't allow; people didn't come out of the reconditioning centres the same. Now the corps had started putting out bounties for old tech dealers it was too dangerous not to be careful. Getting to the site early meant Cled could scope the area out. He climbed the fire escape of a nearby building to get a vantage and look over the nearby streets. It was at a cross-section in the roads allowing a lot of visibility. That was why Cled had picked this spot for the exchange. There were also plenty of escape options.

There was no sign of anyone nearby. If there was they might disrupt the deal or sell information about it to the corps. Many cyber implants had monitoring tech built in. They might just walk by something and not take an interest in it but all the information their implants collected went to the corps. If you did something they didn't like near a cyber they'd send their guards after you. The corps had too much influence and power for local governments to stop them. What they said went. Governments really just organised street cleaning and bin emptying schedules these days. Not that they did a great job of that. Cled checked his wrist. Life is better this way.

About half an hour after Cled arrived his client showed up. Cled descended the fire escape and motioned his client over to meet him in a waste-filled alley. The client who had been using the code name raccoon in their communications with Cled crossed the street to reach Cled. "Can't I set the location," he complained, "Had to get across half the city to get here. Damn buses were cancelled all night."

"No, I always set the location. Otherwise, there's no deal. I have your holomap here. It's all set up look. You press this button here to bring up the holodisplay." Cled explained. Racoon nodded along and seemed to understand. Cled passed him the holomap and he

passed Cled some sparkcoins. Cled
checked them in the palm of his hand.
"All the sparks are there pal." They
were. Cled nodded and the two parted
ways. That was an easy deal. No cybers,
the location was good and the client did
what he was told.

Before he left Cled checked his wrist.
Life is better this way. He pulled out
his holomap and set it for home. He
separated his workshop from his home. It
would be harder for the corps to link
his old tech business to him if they
found the workshop that way. He did have
some old tech at home but it was still
technically legal to keep, just not to
distribute. To get home he had to cross
another district border. This time he
had to climb over two fences blocking
each side of an alley. Soon he was home.
It was 4 a.m., only two hours until his
interview.

Cled tried to sleep but he worried
about his interview, He worried about
not being able to sleep and he worried
about worrying about not being able to
sleep. The interview was important. He
needed a job that would look like it
paid for his apartment. The corp
investigators had been checking his
accounts recently. Cled had stopped

putting his old tech money in and his account was slowly draining. If he couldn't get a job to at least partially offset that there would be further investigations. He may have gotten ten minutes of sleep in those two hours before the interview.

 When cled woke up he checked his wrist. Life is better this way. He quickly dressed and watered his plants since he had been in his workshop for a few days before leaving for the interview. The plants kept the air purity up in his apartment and his workshop and they pulled Cled out of his tech-filled life. Old and new tech could be distracting and these plants had a slower more natural demand. There was no chance Cled would replace his plants with the air purifiers the corps tried to push these days claiming they were more fashionable than plants. That was all just corp propaganda anyway. Once again following his holomap, Cled was making good progress to the building where his interview would be.

 In the morning the streets were busier with commuters but not particularly busy. Cled kept his head down in the hopes no angry brainwashed cybers would harass him. Most of the people in the streets were cybers of one form or another. They all had different implants but the implants all did the same thing in different ways. They all took over your life, they all watched your every move and they were all constantly demanding your attention.

He soon reached what should have been a district border but it wasn't there. No district guards, no border subscription checks and no fences. Cled had forgotten to leave his holomap connected to the network so it could update overnight. He would have to be cautious otherwise he could be caught in a dangerous situation. He continued to follow the holomap. The streets would still mostly be correct but the district borders would definitely have changed. Cled edged his way along toward the interview.

Fortunately, the interview wasn't far. He came across one actual district border but it was still being set up. There was an alley nearby that didn't even have fences up yet that Cled made his way through. With a glance over the shoulder after leaving the alley, Cled was quickly on his way. After that, it wasn't long before Cled got to his interview at Invisiglass. They were a relatively small company, although no company was small these days. Invisiglass manufactured different types of glass. The work was simple, especially for their non-cyber workers but they did take on non-cybers.

The building was a large warehouse which housed the glass manufacturing line, most of which was automatic. When he entered he was waved over to an office in the corner of what was a large very open room with various types of machinery in the centre. Inside he shook hands with his interviewer, a cyber with a right eye implant and a left arm one. Sitting down across from the interviewer Cled exchanged greetings with her. Then the interview began.

Since the work was incredibly simple the interviewer, Cled never got her name, tried to evaluate Cled's character more than anything else. She asked about Cled's commitments and interests first. Then came the inevitable questions. "So why haven't you got any cyber implants yet?" she asked in a shrill voice.

"I find they distract me and diminish my focus. They are undoubtedly useful but I think that distraction isn't worth it." Cled lied.

"I see, " she replied looking down her
nose at information on her arm implant.
"Do you intend to get implants?" she
continued. Cled hesitated for a moment
before replying, "No I don't think so.
As I said they can be distracting." The
interviewer nodded and then looked up
properly from her implant. "I am
sympathetic to you non-cybers. I can't
pretend I understand why you don't get
implants. That doesn't make sense to me.
Yet I also don't agree with you being
pushed to the edges of society and
discarded. You may not be able to
perform some jobs as well as a cyber but
this job does not need cyber reflexes or
calculation speeds. You can have the
job."

 At that Cled relaxed. Finally, he would
not be constantly trying to keep up with
the investigators. Cled got the details
he needed for his very limited shifts
and found out when he would be starting
before leaving Invisiglass. When he got
outside the door he checked his wrist.
Life is better this way. Then he
cautiously followed his holomap home so
he could update it before getting caught
out by the district changes. On his way
home the exhaustion from lack of sleep
had finally hit Cled. After plugging his

holomap in to update when he got back to his apartment he went straight to sleep.

After sleeping for most of the day Cled woke up as it was going dark again. He shook himself awake. What time was it? It was 8. He had a deal to sell an old tech security system at 9. That didn't leave Cled long to get back to his workshop to pick up the system, get to the drop-off point and do his usual checks. Following his holomap Cled quickly made his way to the workshop and then to the drop-off spot. At the workshop, he picked up a new bit of tech he wanted to test as well as the security system. Luckily the district borders were easily avoided.

It was only a few minutes before the agreed meeting time. That made Cled uneasy. He liked to get to the spot early and make sure it was secure. He had been a fool not to set an alarm. At least he'd brought his new device; a new tech scanner. It could search everything within a 20m radius for new tech. Most new tech had components that simply didn't appear in other devices making it somewhat easy to search for. The scanner didn't pick anything up but that didn't entirely ease Cled. He had only tested the device in his workshop so he wasn't quite certain he was safe.

After a few minutes, new tech was detected on the scanner. Cled instantly tensed back up. He couldn't see anyone so he ducked behind a large dustbin. The scanner reported that the new tech had gone. Maybe it was just a cyber passing by. Soon his client arrived. Cled knew his name although he knew Cled as Bauble. This was Rodger a relatively dim-witted man who often broke his old tech. "Hey, Bauble what you doing behind that bin there? You got the system with you?"

Cled didn't answer the first question, Rodger still didn't understand the risks Cled took getting old tech to him. The only reason he hadn't gotten any new tech was that he couldn't keep up with the rate technology was advancing. Cled pulled a camera out of the bag to show Rodger. "It's all in this bag Rodger. It's the usual price" Cled said with a stern face. Rodger began counting out the sparks. "This deal is well worth it, you know Bauble? The corps will buy this stuff off me for like four times what I give you."

Cled put the camera back in the bag. "No deal, don't contact me again. I'm

not trading with someone who gives my
tech to the corps. You fool!" Cled said
cutting Rodger off. "But, but, I'm
paying the price." Rodger stammered.
Cled just shook his head and left. For
one he didn't want the cybers learning
how his tech worked but if Rodger kept
going to them with old tech they would
realise he had a supplier. That would
lead the cyber corps straight to Cled.
Cled had to prevent that at all costs.
He couldn't go to a reconditioning
centre.

Chapter Two

It had been six months since Cled had got the job at Invisiglass and the investigators seemed to have been thrown off. No one had come looking for Cled and he was earning enough money legally to cover his rent. The job was mind-numbingly dull though. Often Cled found himself checking his wrist and being greeted by the tattoo of life is better this way. He began to question if it was when he was working. Cled stood at a conveyor pointing a device at sheets of glass if it beeped the glass had to be taken off the conveyor and thrown in a waste bin. The device checked if the material had any microfractures. It cost less in those days to pay the low wages of a non-cyber than it did for a machine to do some jobs. That was the real reason Invisiglass had hired him. None of these lies about the boss being sympathetic to non-cybers.

There were four non-cybers in the entire warehouse including Cled. They were only used in areas where they worked out cheaper than a machine which wasn't many. Cled had got to know the others and they all seemed like good

people with their own reasons for
avoiding becoming a cyber. Gary was
afraid he wouldn't be able to have kids
which was wrong. The implants had been
indisputably proven not to cause
sterility. Alice was scared of the
technology being used to control her,
especially with implants directly to the
mind. That was something Cled had seen
happen once. Henry just wanted a simple
life which was understandable.

Cled only really saw the others on
breaks since they were spread out across
the warehouse. When they were working
they were generally stuck at their
stations. This added to the monotony
since Cled couldn't even speak to his
co-workers. Yet even with such limited
contact, Cled had managed to make some
great trades with his co-workers and
many of their non-cyber friends too.
Cled's old tech business was booming.

On his way out of the warehouse, Cled
caught up with Henry to talk to him
about a deal he'd arranged with his
friend who was using the codename
Bigtree. All of Cled's colleagues knew
him as Darren so he used this name with
their friends too. Gary was ahead of
them both and slowed down when he heard
them both talking. They both went quiet,

it was best not to let more people know about a deal than needed to. "No need to stop talking for me." Gary said, he hadn't quite grasped the idea yet, "You guys want to grab a drink at the Robot Hound?"

"We'll catch up with you, we're just working something out," Henry explained. He had his head screwed on and also had many non-cyber friends so Cled did a lot of work through Henry these days. After discussing the location, time and what to bring, the two followed Gary to the Robot Hound pub. Since Henry was often a mediator in these deals Cled had allowed him to start setting some of the drop-off locations. Henry knew what Cled needed and Cled had grown to trust him. The money Henry had got from the deals made his simple life a lot more comfortable.

The Robot Hound was a relatively accepting pub. Anyone was allowed in at least, cyber or non-cyber. If you caused a commotion though then it was Big Bill the bartender's choice about what happened to you. He was a cyber in a sense. None of his tech was new tech as Cled would define it. It wasn't constantly linked to the corps and wasn't wired into his mind in the same

way. Bill had lost an arm, but no one
really knew how, he told lots of tales
about how it might have happened and he
had a mechanical replacement. Cled
reckoned that it was a precursor to the
current new tech implants. Either way,
it meant that both cybers and non-cybers
respected Bill and Bill accepted both in
his pub.

Cled hadn't known about such places
before he'd started working at
Invisiglass. There were so many people
here and none of them hated him even the
cybers. If they wanted to or not their
implants still reported back to the
corps though. After getting a round from
the bar the three colleagues sat in a
booth in the corner, furniture
upholstered in a way that was common 50
years prior. How was it that pubs always
seemed to be a time capsule to the past?

"You see the roboball game last night?"
Gary asked. Cled hadn't seen it and he
knew Henry wasn't a fan but before
either of them got a chance to answer
the question Gary proceeded to describe
it, "The Red Destroyer flipped Starlight
just before a touch and Little Walter
managed to return it just in time. Not
seen something like that in a while."
Both Henry and Cled listened patiently

as Gary described the game in great detail. That was about the only thing Gary ever went into detail about. He was obsessed with roboball and was a bit too slow to have gotten into anything else in his life. Still, Cled didn't mind, it was better meeting with his friends in the Robot Hound and being forced into roboball conversation than sitting alone in his apartment.

After chatting a while and a few drinks, one of Cled's phones rang. It wasn't his old tech business phone since that was never on loudspeaker. It was his personal phone. Only one person ever rang him on that; it was Beth. The second time Cled had ever come to the Robot Hound he'd met her. It wasn't long after that they started dating. "Hey C, I was going to ask where you were but from the noise, I can tell you're at the Robot Hound. I'll be there soon," she said and hung up before Cled got a word in. "Is Beth coming," Henry leaned over and asked Cled while Gary was still ranting, "Is Laina with her?" Cled shook his head and whispered back, "I have no clue." They continued their conversation until Beth and Laina showed up.

They all greeted each other. After shuffling around so Beth could sit by

Cled, by some coincidence, Laina was sat very close to Henry. Laina kissed Henry lightly when they'd gotten comfortable. "Still not memorised every tactic those robots have Gary?" Beth asked provoking a laugh from the table. "If you had to get an implant, what would it be?" Laina asked purposefully diverting from roboball but also asking a dangerous question given the current location. "Those ones that make you run super quick." said Gary instantly, "That would save time getting to work."

"You're a fool, Gary, you live across the road from work," Cled said, "I wouldn't have one unless I was forced to, but Big Bill's seems good. No mind control or reporting just simple old technology." Henry nodded his agreement followed by a few yeses from the others. "Well, I'd have one of those new backpacks with all the handy little things in. There's one with an umbrella that automatically pops up when it starts raining." Laina explained unable to hold her answer in any longer, "How about you Henry?"

"They all complicate things. I'd want something simple that didn't distract me too much. Like maybe…"

Beth interrupted before Henry finished his thought, "I wouldn't get anything. They couldn't make me. I don't see any cybers who look happier than non-cybers." Beth had gotten louder as she had spoken and most of the room was looking their way. The five agreed to leave before they had any trouble.

Not too far from the Robot Hound Cled and Beth split off from the rest saying their goodbyes. Cled was happy to have some time alone with her. Beth took Cled to a rooftop she'd found a way up to. There were some old abandoned benches up there that the two sat on. The sky was clear and for Howlchester there was a surprising amount of visible stars. They gazed up at them chatted and cuddled for a while.

Beth had hold of Cled's hand and his wrist was facing upwards displaying his tattoo. She traced the letters with her other hand. "You never really told me what this meant C," Beth said. Cled had been reluctant to explain it when they first met. The tattoo reminded him of hard times so he'd never fully explained it. Truly he had never really explained the tattoo properly to anyone.

"Once I did use new tech," Cled began, "I thought so what if they're watching me? What have I got to hide? I was a fool. It was just a holowatch and I was in the next room. My parents were shouting at the news. It was when cyber corps were first getting real power over laws and how things operated. They barely said anything. Just that it was wrong and that the corps had no right to be in charge, that they hadn't voted for them. My watch was the only new tech in the house so it must have been me, since the next day CyberMe drones came. They used those words that they had said the day before as justification and arrested them. It was not long after that we had their funerals."

"So I swore never again to use new tech but it was hard to quit my holowatch. I kept putting it back on or checking my wrist when it wasn't there. Eventually, I destroyed my holowatch by throwing it into the river but I still kept checking my wrist and being met with disappointment. So I got this tattoo to remind me that what I had done was right. That life was better without new tech in it."

Beth took a few moments to take it in before she looked at him again and said, "That's awful, those wretched corps deserve to be torn down. I'm with you always C. New tech is destroying this world." After that, they moved on to more light-hearted topics of conversation. Beth told him how she'd got the high score on an old arcade machine she'd found after she'd been trying for months and the two talked about everything that had happened since the last time they had seen each other.

When it started to become cold they went back to Cled's apartment. On his way, home Cled realised that maybe he'd finally worked it all out. His cover job was working, his old tech business was booming and with Beth and the others in his life, everything started to feel right again. He wanted this to last forever. After getting back they ate and relaxed for a while. Cled went to sleep early so he could complete the deal he'd discussed with Henry before his work the next day.

In the morning, Cled woke up to his alarm. Beth mumbled about turning it off before turning over and falling back to sleep. It didn't take long for Cled to get ready after which he was straight out of the apartment. He had to pick a few things up from his workshop before the deal. The items he'd agreed to sell were still there and he had Henry's cut

of their last deal stashed there too.
Cled hadn't picked the stuff up the
night before since the workshop was on
the way to the drop-off location.

Cled followed his holomap, as usual, to
his workshop. He'd updated the maps
overnight so there were no border
issues. Only a few months ago Cled had
moved the workshop. One of the Corps had
bought the building the old workshop was
in and had actually noticed the unused
space. Fortunately, Cled had had time to
get his equipment out. Moving workshops
hadn't set Cled back much though, It was
easy to find other space forgotten by
another corporation. They owned so much
that small spaces seemed to be easily
forgotten by them.

After picking up his things from the
workshop Cled moved on to the drop-off
location. He didn't have time to do all
of his usual checks but he had brought
his cyber scanner so he set that up and
waited. He trusted Henry's friends and
knew the area as well as he could know
any area in the ever-changing
Howlchester. The deal was incredibly
smooth. Bigtree turned up, greeted Cled,
gave him the sparks, took the tech and
left.

Nice and simple. Cled was getting too accustomed to that. He'd had no dubious deals, confused customers or run-ins with investigators since starting at Invisiglass and working with Henry. Sometimes he worried he wouldn't be able to handle those things if he had to deal with them again. Cled had plenty of practice in the past; those things wouldn't be a problem if they ever came up again surely.

After the deal, Cled continued on to his work at Invisiglass. Once again he found himself bored at work while checking the microfractures in the glass. He kept finding himself looking at the tattoo on his wrist. Life is better this way. He thought about the previous day and knew it was, but sometimes this work was unbearably dull. He went on checking the glass again and again. Only once that morning did he find a microfracture and get to do something slightly different from scanning the pieces coming along the conveyor. What felt like an eternity later was lunchtime.

At lunch, he sat with the other non-cybers on a small bench to one side of the huge warehouse. Cled sat next to Henry and passed him his cut for the last few jobs under the table while Gary once again blabbered about roboball only this time to Alice. They both knew what Cled and Henry were doing, Cled only passed it under the table to hide the transfer from the cameras.

Just as Henry was taking the money the intercom began echoing through the room startling the whole table. Henry quickly hid the money in his bag. The cybers never said anything on the intercom to them. "This is an announcement to inform all Invisiglass staff that from today we will be merging with Hyperpane. We will take the Hyperpane name and continue to produce the highest quality product."

Cled and Henry both relaxed realising that they hadn't been caught. "Can't believe we're going to have different bosses. That'll be weird." Gary said

"These mergers happen all the time. The internal company barely changes when it is doing well like Invisglass was. The bigger corp just eats the little one so it can continue growing." Cled explained. Henry nodded in agreement and then said, "Still I think we should stop doing anything incriminating at work. We never used to do these swaps here, and with the new owners, we don't know who might be coming to check out their new factories. Plus that scared me I thought we were done for."

"Relax Henry. We weren't caught and I doubt they'll do inspections here for long. I'll get the money to you another way for a while but if they don't add any more cameras or security here then I'll continue to give it to you here. It's much more convenient and we aren't going out of our way to meet for a trade." Henry nodded and they both realised they had just had that conversation too openly. They'd always made sure only those who needed to know knew the full information about trades. Henry quickly changed the conversation by asking Gary who was playing roboball that night.

Chapter Three

Working at Hyperpane turned out to be exactly the same as working at Invisiglass. Cled did the same job of checking for microfractures as he had before. As expected there were a few cybers looking around for the first few weeks but they didn't take long. The manager had changed but was less interested in what the non-cybers were doing than the old manager had been. It wasn't long before everyone settled back into doing exactly what they were doing before. After a few months, Henry was the only one who was acting cautiously still. He refused to take money from Cled at work and he was jumpy.

It was getting close to the end of the day, and Cled kept checking his wrist. Life is better this way. He'd arranged to see Beth after work but needed to pick something up for her first. Time seemed to grind to a halt. The panes of glass travelled achingly slow across the conveyor and all of them were fine so Cled didn't even get to throw any away. It got to what must have been about half an hour before closing and Cled decided to set up the microfracture scanner to point at the conveyor. He put some tape over the scan button and left it. Hyperpane's new manufacturing techniques meant there were practically no fractures anymore but people would notice if the scan number wasn't right.

Cled hurried out of the door passing Gary on the way. "Where are you off to? Work doesn't finish until six. Haven't you already had a warning?" Gary blurted out as Cled passed. He didn't bother answering Gary's questions and instead quickly made his way out of the Hyperpane warehouse. Soon Cled was swapping some old tech for a necklace. The man had arranged the trade location but since this was a one-off Cled had let it slide. The necklace was perfect. Simple with one gem on a plain chain.

Someone passed the stairway where Cled had met his client and Cled jumped. The figure was hooded and Cled couldn't tell if he was a cyber. He had forgotten his scanner for new tech. "Thanks for the necklace," Cled said running from the scene. He couldn't get caught, especially not before he saw Beth. After he was out of sight and around a few corners he relaxed. There was no one around and the deal had been done. Cled had no old tech on him; other than his holomap and his mobiles. If anyone stopped him, they couldn't arrest him for that.

After composing himself, Cled pulled out his holomap so he could make his way to the restaurant where he was meeting Beth. It wasn't long before he was traversing the streets and crossing corp borders as usual. That was until he came across a border that didn't appear on the map. It was the last thing Cled needed. He would be late to meet Beth at this rate. Looking at the guards from Everest, he considered running past. He would be a fool to do that. They'd surely catch him. Apparently, their leg implants gave them superspeed.

Instead, Cled searched around the streets nearby for another way across the border. He found an alley. There was already a new wall up to the height of the buildings on either side. Someone entered a block of flats that was on the border. Cled dashed in before the automatic door slowly closed. Cled had hoped there would be another opening at the other end of the building but the end of the corridor was just a brick wall. He made his way upstairs where he found a window that opened onto the other side of the border. Fortunately, the window was open. It was only a one-floor drop. It might hurt a little but it would be nothing major. Cled hung by his hands out of the window and let himself fall.

He felt the impact hard on his legs. He was fine. It didn't take him long after that to reach the restaurant. Gacho's was the restaurant's name. Henry had said it was good and very welcoming to non-cybers. They focused on fusion cuisine which sounded good from what Henry had said. When Cled got inside, Beth was already sitting at the table. He hurried over while taking his coat and bag off. "Sorry Beth, I got caught by a border change. damn Everest."

"Don't worry about it C, you're here now. I've not been to a restaurant in years. I didn't even know there were any left that welcomed non-cybers."

"This place is pretty fancy. I didn't know either; Henry recommended it. He said to get the Chinese-African fusion dishes. They're the best ones they do here." The two ordered and got exceptionally polite service which Cled didn't trust. Even in places that only welcomed non-cybers people weren't that friendly. Never mind a restaurant that was mostly filled with cybers greeting Cled like he was one of them.

When the food came it was incredible. It tasted like nothing Cled had ever tried before and he couldn't think of anyone better to share it with than Beth. They had a good time and after eating stayed for a few drinks even though Cled had a job later that evening. "You never bring me anywhere like this C, I know we don't exactly have many options, what's the occasion?"

"I just wanted you to know how much you mean to me, Beth. Since I've known you my life has been so much better." Cled held Beth's hand across the table while presenting the necklace to her with the other. "C you mean the world to me too. This necklace is beautiful. Where did you get it?"

"I couldn't reveal my secrets, Beth. Are you going to try it on?" Beth undid the clasp and put the necklace around her neck. It looked perfect on her and Cled told her so. After another drink, they left Gacho's and began making their way back to Cled's apartment. Cled was suddenly aware of how much time must have passed and checked the time. He didn't have long before his next deal. Luckily they weren't too far from the workshop. "I didn't realise the time. I've got to do this deal and then I'll

see you back home." Cled began parting
from Beth.

 "Be safe C, I love you." Cled turned,
smiled and said,

 "I love you too Beth." Before running
in the direction of his workshop.

 Getting to his workshop with the
outdated holomap wasn't much of an issue
for Cled but when he did get there he
didn't have time to update the map
before leaving for the deal. At the
workshop, he quickly picked up the
holomaps he had agreed to sell. Cled
didn't have much trouble navigating to
the location of the deal either. There
were a few more border changes. All of
them were relatively easy to avoid this
time though.

 The deal was under an overpass which
had been wedged between two skyscrapers.
Cled hadn't picked up his scanner for
new tech again so he had a quick scout
of the area himself. He didn't notice
anything unusual in the short time
before his client showed up. The client,
whom Cled knew as Jimmy, was a regular
so he wasn't too worried.

 "Hey Darren, you got the stuff?" Jimmy
announced with his nasal voice as he
entered the area under the overpass.
Cled originally knew Jimmy through Henry

so he Knew Cled as Darren. Cled had begun doing some business like this without Henry though since Henry had become far more cautious recently. "You know I have them, Jimmy. What do you need new maps for anyway? Don't all your crew already have them?"

"I don't need any maps Cled. I'm here for you." Jimmy lowered his hood revealing an eye implant. Looking more closely he also had a wrist one. "You ratted on me. Jimmy, you fool!"

"I don't feel so foolish with these implants. I'm stronger and smarter than ever. The way I see it you're hindering progress and so was I until I got these implants. The cybers are right Cled." Cled wasn't talking his way out of this. He turned to run but hooded figures emerged from Cled's planned escape route. He looked around and couldn't see where to go. The cybers closed on him. The building windows. Cled slammed his body through one of the windows to the building on either side of the overpass. The cybers pursued.

"You can't escape us Cled, you must know that," Jimmy called after him. Cled frantically made his way through the building looking for a way out. They were a few floors up from the bottom of

the building. Cled found some stairs and
rushed down. There was the door. Cled
ran for it. A lift to his side opened as
Cled passed. One of the cybers was
inside. He lunged for Cled. Hoping over
the hooded figure's arm Cled made it to
the building door.

 He didn't know where he was. Running
Cled pulled out a holomap. He set it for
the coordinates of his workshop. Maybe
Cled could hold them off there.
Following the map, Cled was able to lose
his pursuers. Then he came across a
VidTube border. That wasn't on the map.
The guards saw Cled stop running and
turn around. They were suspicious. Cled
darted off as quickly as he could before
arousing more trouble. The hooded cybers
turned the corner Cled had just come
from.

 Cled ran down the street staying within
the border desperately hoping for
another way across. Both the guards and
the other cybers were chasing him now.
There was an alley with only a chainlink
fence. Cled could get over that. Cled
scrambled up. He was at the top. His
pursuers tried to grab at him but he'd
got over. They shouted after him as he
ran. He couldn't stop now although his
lungs protested against the continued

exertion. At the end of the alley, guards were already coming to intercept him. Cled ducked underneath their grasp. He was lucky Vidtube guards didn't have speed implants.

Cled began following the holomap again. He ran as hard as he could. Turning down a street, he found a wall too high to get over. He looked around for any other way to go. The only way out was the way Cled had come. He threw the holomap to the floor as he was surrounded by the Vidtube guards and the hooded cybers who were with Jimmy. They threw Cled to the ground and began beating him. Kicking him. Punching him. None of them asked any questions they just hated Cled. Cled was helpless. He squirmed and wriggled but couldn't get free. It wasn't long before Cled lost consciousness.

Chapter Four

Since Cled had no way of measuring time
in the windowless room they'd put him
in, he'd started measuring it by the
beatings. Often Cybers would come to
kick and punch Cled until he no longer
reacted to the impact of their metallic
limbs. Some were the same every time.
Others were outsiders brought in by
their friends on the security teams.
Somehow it had become a pass-time to
beat non-cybers without any real reason.
They all just wanted to hurt Cled, never
asking him questions. Never even looking
at his face.

In some ways, the beatings were better
than the time between them. Between Cled
truly felt the pain they had caused.
When the cybers were there they hurt
Cled, but the constant ache, the
unrelenting pain after was what got to
him. Every movement sent waves of hurt
through Cled's body. What was worse
though was it slowly felt a little
better and just as it felt like Cled
could heal another beating would come.
This cycle continued for a long time.
There were at least a hundred beatings.
Cled was being fed but he didn't
remember that.

Between the beatings, Cled thought
about before, at least when he was
conscious. Before cybers, when the world
was simpler. When no one had to decide
if they should modify themselves or not.
That always led to thoughts of how
things changed though. Initially, cybers
weren't given jobs. People thought that
their implants were spying on them or
that cybers were somehow cheating.
People hated them because they were
different, they didn't trust them. Cled
had never understood their hatred of
them then. Yes, all the data they
recorded was sent back to the corps but
it wasn't the person's fault.

After a while, people started to
realise the benefits of having cybers
working for them. They were incredibly
efficient. Direct connections to the
brain containing the entire internet
meant a cyber could learn anything in an
instant. Improved Strength and mobility
meant they could do a better job than
most non-cybers. Soon Businesses lost
their edge if they didn't have a cyber
on the team because all of their
competitors did. Soon it became a race.
Whoever had the most cybers was on top.
Those businesses became the cyber corps
that grew to dominate the world. They

were unshakable giants that could not be stopped.

By the time the corps took over the script had flipped. With all the cyber's minds linked they seemed like some sort of hivemind. The pains that had been inflicted on the few when people didn't understand them were now directed back at any non-cybers but magnified tenfold. Instead of peace, it felt like the cybers wanted revenge. All Cled had wanted was to go on being himself. He didn't want to change his body or his mind. He didn't want to join a hive mind that had somehow decided it was okay to kill his parents for privately disagreeing with the way they took over the world.

For being himself, he was punished. First, came sly comments. Then the comments were open and overt, people allowed them because the cybers had been unjustly treated. Then came straight-out attacks. Many non-cybers hid themselves to avoid such conflict as Cled had for so long. Then most cybers seemed to just stop caring. Cled had felt freer than he had for years just before he'd been caught by the cybers that had him. These cybers were worse than any Cled had encountered. Every shred of their power

seemed to go towards their hate of
non-cybers.

What was the point? Why be so angry at
someone who had never harmed you? All
Cled had done was make and sell
technology that didn't benefit the corps
anymore. Barely anyone even bought it.
He'd never hurt anyone. He just also
never did anything that benefited the
cyber corps. He didn't believe they
helped the world and why should he? The
extra productivity from cybers had not
created a better world. It was the same
with a few nice gadgets. Only one thing
had increased and that was anger. At
first against cybers and now non-cybers.
This technology had changed the world
for the worse.

For so long Cled had thought he had
been resisting and that he was somehow
preventing this change. That was how he
had begun to have a better life before
he had been caught. Now he realised that
wasn't true, people like him had become
so few that the cyber corps no longer
cared so much. Cled was one of the last
of a dying group. The last time he had
met another old tech dealer was years
ago, maybe he was the last one.

After many more beatings, a cyber came
alone whom Cled had never seen before.

He moved slowly around Cled, watching him and waiting. After a while, Cled found the effort to slump himself up against the wall and get a proper look at the cyber. The man had more implants than any cyber Cled had ever seen. There was more metal than skin. Over his implants, the man was smartly dressed in a long waistcoat over the top.

 "They call you dealers threats to society," the man said with perfect pronunciation, "Yet all I see is scum. Most people would not even give you a first look when passing never mind a second. At one time a threat to society actually could do some damage to our network. They could hurt us instead of just feeding off our waste." Cled didn't have anything to say. This cyber was clearly an investigator. It seemed he was here to give Cled a verbal beating but after so many physical ones Cled was happy to just listen.

 "A quiet one." the investigator said leaning in close to Cled's face, "They are going to send you to one of our rehabilitation centres. It is more than you deserve if you ask me, why would we want to integrate someone like you into our society? Anyway, before you go I wanted you to know that we always knew.

Our algorithms picked your actions out years ago as a dealer, we just never got a good opportunity to apprehend you. With Gary there collecting evidence we had enough to kill you in the streets and get away with it. No no, they said. Let's do this properly."

The investigator paused for a moment. Cled realised that Gary's actions had been odd. He'd been a fool to let Gary know so much. All along Cled had just thought Gary was a fool but no he'd played him. "So here we are," The inspector continued, "Soon you'll be a cyber just like the rest of us. It will not take you long to accept it either. More than you deserve as I said. Goodbye Cled, enjoy the centre. You will be there for quite some time."

The investigator slowly turned away from Cled and left. He moved so slowly, if Cled had been less weak he could have gotten in an easy attack on the cyber from behind or have run out of the cell. Yet with his implants, Cled likely wouldn't have gotten very far. Not long after the investigator left some cybers entered the cell that Cled recognised. Cled flinched but they were not here to beat him and instead dragged Cled away.

They threw Cled in the back of a van, slammed the door shut and began driving. As they went Cled was flung around the vehicle having no seatbelt and nothing to hold on to in his weak condition. He didn't know for how long they drove and couldn't tell where they were going. The inside of the windowless van was as dark as the cell they'd had Cled in. Eventually, the vehicle stopped. The doors opened revealing daylight and the cybers faces. They dragged him out and into a courtyard.

The yard was massive. Cled looked around to see an old country house and some beautiful gardens. This place looked like it hadn't been touched by the constant growth and expansion the cyber corps forced upon Howlchester. Cled didn't get a chance to see much more before he was pulled inside the building. The insides were ornately detailed but Cled focused on the sign above where they took him, it read: transitioning centre. Cled was put in another cell-like room and left there.

This cell was far more accommodating than the previous one. There were lights and windows, even though they were barred, and the whole room was lighter. There was a bed and a toilet. All these things gave Cled a sense of dread. If they were giving him these things he would be here for a long time. Cled checked his wrist, "Life is better this way."

Sometime later a woman came with only a few very basic cyber implants. "Hello darling," she said very calmly, "I'm here to ask you some preliminary questions." The woman had little to defend herself from Cled but Cled no longer had the energy in him to do anything, so he went along with the woman's questioning. "I'm Nurse Amanda, I'll be your transitioner while you're here. You look quite beat up, would you say that you are of sound mind?" Cled nodded.

"No darling, I need you to say it." She said in her ear-piercing upbeat tone. "Yes, I'm of sound mind." Cled droned. "Okay, that's good." She looked closer at Cled, "We'll get those wounds attended to for you later. Will you agree to get a neural implant?" Cled began frantically shaking his head, "No I will not!"

"It's nothing to worry about darling, we can use the implant to nullify your pain. The quicker we get you one the quicker you'll be able to leave too. If

you agree we can let you straight back
out into society. You could go back to
your normal life."

 "I said no. You can't make me have an
implant. I refuse." Cled shouted into
Amanda's face. She tutted at him and
began leaving the room. Just before she
left she turned and looked at Cled. "I
think you'll find we can make you and we
will."

 A similar thing happened day after day.
Nurse Amanda would come in and be nice,
calling cled "darling" and tending to
his wounds. Slowly she would start to
bring up the idea of implants, how they
would benefit Cled, and how he could
leave if he had one, especially a brain
one. A few times Cled was on the edge of
accepting but then he remembered his
parents and why he had never got an
implant in the first place.

 The nurse knew when he was close to
accepting she pushed harder on those
days. They were looking after Cled, he
was healing, and the offer seemed
genuine. The implant wouldn't hurt. They
sold them legally on street corners with
easy attach mechanisms, there was no
major operation. No, they would use the
implant to control him, and Cled would
no longer be Cled. He would become part

of their hive mind. He would accept why they killed his parents, he was no fool. Time and time again Cled refused, they wore him down by asking him over and over and yet he still did not accept.

Eventually, Amanda came with others, Cled did not know how long he'd been in the transitioning centre at that point but he had been there a long time. He had grown a beard on what had been his cleanly shaven face, all of his wounds had healed and he felt well of the body even if not of the mind. "It seems to be that you'll never accept a brain implant, Cled. Fortunately, we can use other methods to convert you." The two who had entered with Amanda stepped toward Cled with what looked like an arm implant installer. "No!" Cled shouted, "I refuse you can't make me." The men grabbed hold of Cled and held him. He tried to wriggle and escape but he could not.

"We can Cled. Any non-brain implant can be installed without a recipient's agreement. Of course we can't let you go freely afterwards until you've adjusted which wouldn't have been an issue with a brain implant." Cled was thrust into a chair. One man held his arm while another held the cold metal of the installer against it. Cled managed to slip his arm free but the man just grabbed his arm again tighter. The installer was on his skin again. All Cled could do was cry out and beg them to stop but they did not. With the press of a button, a metal device clamped itself around Cled's arm. There was a short sharp pain as the device burrowed into Cled's body and then the pain stopped.

"Now you're one of us, darling," Amanda said and the three left Cled alone. He looked at his wrist and saw the implant next to his tattoo, "Life is better this way." That tattoo was wrong. Cled had become what he had strived not to. He was annoyed but the implant didn't make him feel any different. It had a Holo projector and a few buttons. Overall it was not dissimilar to the holowatch he had once worn on that arm. Cled looked for a way to remove the device from his wrist even though he knew there wasn't one. Implants weren't designed to be removed, just upgraded.

There was nothing Cled could do now. He switched the projector on to see what the device did. Instantly Cled was assaulted by a barrage of information. There were banners advertising how he could take this all in far better with the latest brain implant and how human eyes were inferior to it. Underneath the banners were various selectable icons. One was a connection to the network where cybers could discuss things online. Another was some form of work app which looked to award points for finding and categorising sites online. Many others had padlocks displayed next to them with the same points symbol and a number. It looked as if these icons were unlocked by spending the points.

Scrolling through there were hundreds of them. Some looked more like games, while others were different work apps or more niche versions of the network. Far enough through the list were options to buy implants with very high point costs. There were even some icons that were question marks with a description explaining that you had a chance to unlock some of the rarest apps or even implants by spending your points on them. This of course wasn't guaranteed. Cled shut the projector off. He hated it already. They had taken the elements of the old holowatches that hooked people and amplified them.

Sometime later some other cybers came. Cled had always thought of cybers as something other but now he realised he was one. It was really the corps and these manipulative systems they created that were the problem. Cled hadn't been accepted yet either way. They grabbed him and pushed him all the way to another wing of the building. This one was labelled: Societal Rehabilitation Clinic. The two who had held Cled had the same looks on their faces as the cybers who had beaten him in the cell before. They resented Cled, maybe they thought the same as the inspector had. Someone like cled didn't deserve to be brought into "their society."

  After going through a few sets of doors which were locked behind them, they got into the main section of the reconditioning centre. It was large and open with a mostly communal area with rooms on the sides that looked to just have beds. Most of the inmates were sitting in the communal area working on apps on holoprojections from their arm implants. Others conversed and some ate. There seemed to be food machines that could be operated on one side of the room at any time. The whole place had an open feel with comfy seating and lots of light. Other than bars on the window like in Cled's last cell, you would think this was the office of a top cybercorp.

In the room, the guards freed their grip on Cled and pushed him into the centre of the room before making a quick exit. Cled's implant made a beeping sound to notify him of a change. He looked to reveal a time in the top right of the projection that looked to be a countdown. It was for five years. Next to it, there was a little symbol representing "or" and a large image of one of the brain implants with a point cost. It seemed like Cled had two options to leave this place. He either did his time or bought his way out by getting enough points and accepting a brain implant, it seemed that option was no longer free of charge.

Chapter Five

Cled began by getting acquainted with his new home. Most of the inhabitants barely even looked up from their implants at their new cellmate as he roamed around. First, he went over to the food machines. There was one free option for food and one free option for drinks. All the others had point costs next to them but Cled had no idea what points were worth yet so he didn't pay much attention to them. The only thing he did notice was that the values seemed to increase exponentially as you went down the list.

Having access to food when he liked it for the first time in forever; Cled tried out the free option for food and got a drink with it too. The drink was just water which Cled didn't mind but the food was some awful brown insipid slop. It was too thin to be a soup but not thick enough to have any real texture and tasted like the main components of the dish were cardboard and sawdust. Not being certain how consistent his meals would be, Cled continued to eat the slop anyway.

He'd found a seat by the side of the room with the barred windows where he could see the whole room. There he watched as his cellmates went about their lives. They spent most of their time working away on their implants. When they weren't doing that they were eating, drinking, sleeping or doing something for leisure on their implants. They conversed very little verbally but seemed to discuss things on the network, if that was with each other or people outside Cled couldn't tell but he could see the giant logo unmistakably at the top of the holoprojections.

Cled tried talking to one of his cellmates who was sitting at the same table, "Hey, I'm new here."

"Okay." the man grunted.

"What's your name, have you been here long?" Cled asked. "You should get to work on your implant. You'll get out quicker and life is easier with points." The man said ignoring Cled's questions. After that, Cled tried to speak to a few more people but got practically the same response. After a while, he looked down at his watch considering turning it on but read his tattoo, "Life is better this way," and decided against it

At around 9 in the evening, the lights went off in the main room and little lights above the side rooms said the

names of different inmates. Everyone
seemed to stand up at the same time and
walk straight to their room although
there seemed to be nothing forcing them
to do so. Cled stayed sat for a few
minutes and then decided to do the same
as the others since he was tired anyway.
His implant made a little jingle and the
projector turned on by itself. Some
fireworks were projected on the screen
and a point score came up of 9800
points. After pressing ok a table came
up with a review of how all the points
had been earned. 10000 points for ending
the day and -200 for entering the room 2
minutes after the end of the day. 0
points in all the other categories.
These included work, high scores on game
apps and even interest from banked
points.

  Cled continued like that for a few
days. He ate the free food and drank the
water but every day they seemed to taste
worse. Seeing people with better food
and drinks frustrated Cled. He couldn't
even see the value in the things they
were doing to pay for these upgrades. He
found one inmate who occasionally would
talk to him called Jonathan. Jon said
little but he was at least friendly with
Cled. He said "Hello" when they passed

each other and very occasionally he would have a conversation with Cled while still doing something on his projector. It was better than nothing but it didn't fill the day and it only briefly stopped Cled's growing boredom.

After about a week Beth visited for the first time. "Hey C, it took me ages to persuade them to let me in. Are you okay? How'd they get you?"

"It's good to see you, Beth," Cled said with some relief. If he could see Beth then maybe that would get him through his stay here. "I was a fool. I got sloppy and wasn't as careful as I used to be. You're wearing the necklace."

"Of course I am Cled. I'll wait for you to get out. How long have they got you in here for?" She asked clearly hopeful. Cled had kept his arm under the table partially out of shame. He revealed it with a gasp from Beth. "They forced this on my arm. I haven't really used it yet but there's various work apps on it. I either have to stay here for five years or earn enough points and buy a brain implant. I'm not going to do the latter." Cled said with a sigh. "How can they do this C? Surely it isn't even legal to force an implant on someone." Cled shook his head slowly and said,

"They weren't allowed to force a brain implant but I think they can force the others now. They tried for a long time to make me agree to get a brain one. If I had said yes even under their prodding then I'd have one now."

After that, they discussed what was going on outside. How Henry and Laina were and that Gary had been a rat. Then they just sat for a while until on guard came and said Beth had to go. "I love you C," Beth said as she left. Cled said it back before being escorted back to the room where all of his cellmates were working away on their implants.

For a time, Beth came to see Cled at least once a week, but then she got a new job. The place where she was working had been merged with a particularly anti-non-cyber company called Dentine. Beth had found another job but it required long hours for her to keep the job. It had been weeks since Beth had last come although she had got word to him that she would be there today. Cled waited at a table in the middle of the open area for the guards to call him for his visit. It had been months and Cled still hadn't given in and used his implant other than the forced point total pop-up every evening. The others had thought him stupid at first but now his cellmates had seemed to come to respect it. They no longer sniggered when they saw him just sitting around at least anyway. Beth never turned up that day.

The next day Beth did show up. She wore the necklace Cled had given her like she always did. The two had a usual conversation about what each of them had been doing and what their friends were up to, and then it moved on to Laina being pregnant. "It's so irresponsible of her to have kids don't you think Cled?" Beth asked.

"What do you mean irresponsible? What's wrong with having kids?"

"Well the world is awful these days and it's falling apart anyway. Plus there's this new thing where we can upload our brains to the cloud. Then we live in this online space. We'd use lots fewer resources that way, but if people keep having kids it'll be overcrowded." Beth explained.

This was a lot for Cled to take in. It sounded like the corps were planning on controlling people's entire realities not just their minds. He would never give himself up to them so this would not stop him from wanting children.

"Isn't that just another way for the corps to control people though? Imagine if instead of bombarding people with information only when they choose to turn their implants on they are continuously enveloped in what the corps want you to believe."

"Don't be silly C. This isn't made by the corps. We have to do this. Can't you see this will put everyone on an equal playing field with the same abilities and options and we won't be such a drain on the world anymore."

"Who would even be able to fund something like that if it wasn't one of the corps though? It may sound like equality but what happens when they start restricting access and forcing you to pay to gain the ability to use the new technologies they create?" Cled said with frustration in his voice.

"That isn't going to happen I trust them. They're going to fix everything." Beth shouted. Then they were both silent for a while. "So you don't want to have kids with me then Beth?" Cled asked quietly. Beth just shook her head. "And you're going to join this new world?" Beth nodded and said, "When I can, but it sounds like it's years away when it will be done." The two sat in silence

for a while like the first time Beth had
visited. This time it wasn't to stay
near each other though but more to think
over what the other had said. After a
while, Beth got up and said "Goodbye C,
I'll see you when I can." Cled responded
with a halfhearted goodbye.

   After that Beth visited less often and
their conversations were harder to
maintain when she did. She had stopped
wearing the necklace Cled had given her.
Over time she visited less and less and
then eventually she stopped coming
altogether. They never did agree about
brain uploading and kids. Their views on
other things had also begun to drift
apart, but she was the only thing Cled
had anymore so their distance didn't
stop her absence from hurting. For a
while, Cled held on to the hope that she
might come back again and then he gave
up on that. Still, this did not break
his resolve; he refused to give in and
use his implant. He found himself
constantly bored, worse than he had ever
been working at Invisiglass. There was
absolutely nothing in this prison for
Cled to focus on or do, so Cled did
nothing.

   Eventually, months after Cled had last
seen Beth, a message came from her via a

guard. Apparently, she had called and
said she was sorry but she had to break
things off. The emotion was lost in the
guard's gruff uncaring tone but the
message still hit Cled like a truck. His
entire body slumped. He had thought he
had gotten over it, but he must have had
some hope that Beth would come again
hidden within the depths of his body.
For days Cled just lay in his cell
thinking about Beth, about the quiet
moments they'd spent together before he
had been caught. How had they gone from
agreeing on everything about the world
and especially cybers to this
disagreement on the brain uploads? Cled
just didn't understand.

  Cled thought about his entire past,
everything leading up to him being in
this prison. He thought about what had
gotten him here. How things had gone
wrong. He thought about losing his
parents and then about his holowatch.
That had brought him joy. If they had
never killed his parents Cled would
probably have become a cyber. None of
this would have happened then. Cled
looked at his wrist, which he'd been
avoiding doing since he had become a
cyber, and saw his implant next to his
tattoo, "Life is better this way." Cled

laughed out loud. The tattoo seemed so
absurd now. Next to his implant, it felt
as if it was beckoning him and telling
Cled to use it. Cled turned on the
projector and booted up the one work app
that he had access to.

Chapter Six

It had been a few weeks since Cled had started using the projector. He found it hard to see why he had resisted for so long. The work was easy and rewarding. It was mostly answering surveys or sorting files but some bits even felt like games. Every time you made progress you got a little confetti explosion on the right of your screen and thousands of points. It felt good and no matter what Cled did on his implant he was getting more points. Even the games and non-work apps rewarded points. No longer was Cled bored and the room he was in no longer felt like a prison. He wasn't confined when he used his implant. He could talk to people through the Network and he could access practically anything he needed to.

At first, Cled thought the different foods and drinks at the vending machines were a waste of points. You couldn't save if you kept spending. Then after looking at the points scores Cled realised how ridiculously cheap they were. It cost him fewer points than he got for getting back into his bedroom on time to buy pretty good meals for the day. There were more expensive options, some incredibly so, but there were ones that only cost a little bit more and tasted much better and Cled was making way more points than the little extra cost.

At any moment Cled wasn't eating or sleeping, he was looking at the projections from his implant. It was a waste of his time not to. There were all those points he could be earning. Every time he looked he saw his tattoo and for the first time in a long time he actually agreed with it: "Life is better this way." Cled had been a fool not to become a cyber. He'd been resisting this for so long but now it felt so right. Why would anyone not become one when there were just so many benefits?

People in the centre other than Jonathan would talk to Cled now. They never said much but neither did Cled. They all knew that there were more important things to be doing. A polite, "Hello" or "Excuse me" was usually the extent of conversation but they didn't need to say much more in person. It made more sense to talk through the Network anyway since you got points for doing that.

For the first few weeks after Cled had started using the projector, he had intended not to buy the brain implant. It was too invasive and he couldn't see how it would be any better than his arm implant. Now he realised that was silly, he'd seen videos of how efficient people could be at earning points with a brain implant and implants no longer seemed like a problem. Cled's life would just be better with a brain implant that's how things were now. The videos on the Network of people using them proved that. In a lot of the games, people had them too and the people with them were practically super-human, who wouldn't want that?

The lights went off for the end of the day and Cled quickly made his way to his bedroom so he didn't lose any points. The explosion today was massive with hundreds of thousands of points displayed on the table. Today had been a good day for Cled. At this rate, he would be able to buy a brain implant years before he would be released without buying one. If he had started getting points earlier he would have been out even quicker. What a fool he had been to hold out on using his implant for so long.

At night they were not allowed to use their implants so all you could do in

the cells was sleep or think. Cled had
found it hard to sleep recently, his
mind was too focused on optimising how
he could make more points. That resulted
in Cled spending more time thinking than
sleeping. When he had thought things
through as much as he could he still
couldn't sleep though, he was tired but
he just couldn't sleep so his thoughts
drifted to other things.

After being connected to the network,
Beth's comments on mind uploading did
not seem so bad. Cled had not seen her
in a long time and maybe that had been
caused by Cled being a fool. Yet that
did not matter now, there was no way for
Cled to contact her and she probably
would not care even if he could.

Eventually, each night Cled would get
frustrated at his lack of sleep and
would turn on what he had done in the
day. He had fallen into their trap and
he only accepted it because they had
control of him with this awful implant.
He did not know which thoughts were his
own and which had been forced upon him
by the constant bombardment of
information from the terrible device.
Dawn or sleep always arrived before Cled
reached the natural conclusion of these
thoughts. This allowed Cled to return to

using his implant which he simply could
not help. After this, he came to accept
it again throughout the day.

This cycle eventually began to feel
more like torture at night time than any
physical harm that he had received. Why
did they restrict access to the implants
in such a way that made the inmates want
more when they could not have it until
the next day? Why did Cled want it so
much when he had despised it so much in
the past? Why did he want it so much
when he despised it now? It did not make
sense to Cled but there was nothing he
could do about it. He was no longer in
control of himself or his body. All he
had left was fleeting thoughts at night
when the implant's power receded.

Cled's awareness began to give him more
time in control at night. He tried to
think about ways out of this horrible
cycle of euphoric but empty days and
restless nights but the other Cled
fought back. Daytime Cled would not
allow anything to harm his high point
streak and pushed back. Suddenly even in
the night, Cled began to feel like he
was just a passenger in this other
Cled's body. He wanted to scream out but
could not. He was not in control
anymore.

For a while Cled accepted that there was nothing he could do now and just gave up control. What was the point? A non-cyber was fighting a losing battle in this world anyway. Then he could not stand it. He could not stand the point system used to exploit people's brains to use the implants, he could not stand the repetition and he could not stand how being a cyber had been forced upon him and the wider population.

With great willpower, Cled continuously fought against this other force controlling his brain. He did not relent and bit by bit Cled got back more control of his brain. He had pockets of time in the night where he was in control. This was enough for Cled to find a way. He thought and thought and realised all he needed was time. So Cled continued to fight for more and more control of his mind.

It was not easy. For periods the other him pushed Cled in to the background and for others, Cled dominated for most of the day. This invisible war in Cled's mind was waged for months and for so long it seemed like Cled would never take enough back to make his final blow and win once and for all. Then he gained control for a week. That would be enough if he could do it again but there was no way of knowing if he could. No, he knew this would work. It had to work.

He took a knife with him back to his cell, it was incredibly blunt but Cled would make it work. He held his breath and took the knife to his arm with the implant on just below the elbow. There he would cut the implant off without losing his whole arm. This was the only way. There was no way under or around the implant, it went into his flesh and bone. The only way to remove it was to remove the arm it was attached to. Knowing this did not stop the pain.

Through flesh and tendons Cled sawed. Blood spurted at first but then the flow slowed. It was agony but that did not stop Cled's determination. The only way to stop the implant from controlling him was to remove it entirely. Without being attached it would not function. It took time and before he even reached bone his right arm, which he used to cut, ached. Cled did not remember much after that until the arm with the implant still attached dropped to the ground with a thud. He shivered with the pain of his arm but he was satisfied. Now when the other Cled took control there would be nothing he could do. The implant would no longer pull Cled further down that path.

Even knowing the implant was no use without being connected to a person Cled stomped upon it. He let out all of his rage. He had never wanted to be a cyber and this had made him one, it had made him what he had vowed never to become when his parents died. Worst of all he had come to accept it and even like it for a while. What the corps were doing was unacceptable. He hated them, he hated all of this. He caught a last glimpse of the tattoo on his arm, "Life is better this way," and then he blacked out. He lost complete control of himself for a while. He was not even a passenger he had been hidden away in the boot and did not know what was happening for a time.

When Cled awoke again everything was calm. He was in his cell, his arm had been taken away and the blood cleaned leaving the room sterile. He strode out into the common area, no one even blinked. The other inmates had gone back to entirely ignoring Cled, it seemed, but other than that they did not care about his lack of an arm. Cled ordered a water and a bowl of slop triumphantly. They no longer had control of him and without the implant, they could never control him. Cled just hoped they wouldn't force another one upon him.

It didn't take long for Cled's triumph to wear off and for the bordem to set in. There was absolutely nothing to do in this prison without an implant. That was more apparent now after Cled had spent so much time using the implant. Before he had used it, he didn't understand the benefits of the implant and it was easy to forget about it. Now he couldn't easily. His thoughts often drifted to optimising point gains on the apps that he could no longer access. The frequency of those thoughts dwindled over time but when they came up they still hurt.

Cled kept expecting the other him to take over. Maybe he would come back and request a new implant and try and force Cled back into being a cyber again. Nothing like that ever happened though. Cled's life became very quiet and straightforward. Eventually, he came to terms with this and realised he'd been in this prison for over a year and a half. That meant he only had three and a half years left. That wasn't so bad, was it? With the point goals distracting him Cled had never really thought about how little time he actually had to spend here. Five years wasn't such a long time.

That implant had restricted his thoughts so much that he hadn't seen things clearly. He couldn't believe he'd wanted the brain implant, that he'd cared so much about getting out only a little bit earlier. He'd put all of his thoughts into these pointless apps that had no long term benefit for him. When he got out, Cled would move far away to the countryside out of the cyber dominated cities and find somewhere quiet. Then he could just be, maybe he could make a little old tech on the side but nothing major. He would be more free than he had ever been in Howlchester that way.

Although Cled felt as lonely as he ever had, he had a greater feeling of purpose. Beth had left him and he had no way to contact his friends. The cybers were like drones going about their work without a care for him. Yet Cled hadn't given in to the brainwashing that these drones accepted. Diligently working they buzzed about the prison while Cled sat with a free mind. He thought about where he would live when he left, how he would manage, and what he would do. He realised he hadn't been out of the city since before the cyber corps took over and longed to see it. Slowly, his plans grew and his anticipation for his new life grew with them. All he had to do was wait.

Chapter Seven

After the five long years of Cled's imprisonment, most of which were very uneventful, he was finally released. It was a relief to finally leave the doors that he had been forced through all those years ago. Many of the workers there watched as he left. Nurse Amanda and many of the guards were there with looks of disgust on their faces. They had failed to change Cled and it appeared that didn't happen often with those who left. Fortunately, it seemed there was nothing they could do. Ever since Cled had removed his arm they had never tried to force another implant upon him. There must have been some rule against it that the corps hadn't managed to get around yet.

After Cled got outside of the grounds, the guards pushed him out onto the road and left him there. With only the clothes on his back and without his left arm, Cled didn't know what to do. There was no way he would be able to navigate Howlchester now. Without a holomap and with likely countless changes to the winding network of intersections that was the city he would stand little chance at getting to any of his stashes inside. After walking down the road for a while Cled remembered a stash that he had left out of town. That must have been over a decade ago now, there probably wouldn't be a holomap there but there could be something he could use.

The stash wasn't so far, it was a little overgrown but Cled managed to clear the roots off the entrance to the small pit where the stash was. It was really just a small hole which Cled could just about fit inside. There he had stored an old tech phone, some money and some long life food. The food tasted better than the slop he had been eating and he quickly got through a portion. After that, he looked through the contact list on the phone for anyone he might be able to trust. Almost everyone in there were clients or people Cled had stopped working with long before he had been captured. No Henry or Laina and no Beth.

Beth! Cled remembered her number but it had been so long and they hadn't left things on the best of terms. He thought about it for a while and then decided Beth was the only person he could call if he wanted to go back into Howlchester and maybe recover his things. He had no intention of staying in the city again

but it would be much easier to start
again if he had some of his old tech and
the money he had made from selling it.
Maybe he could reconcile with Beth too.
Although he had put Beth to the back of
his mind while he was imprisoned, he
still cared about her. Could they start
fresh too?

"C? Is that you?" Beth asked after Cled
said hello.

"It's me Beth, are you doing okay?"
Cled asked cautiously. "You're lucky I
still have this old thing C, I got rid
of a lot of my old tech not too long
back. I never got around to getting rid
of the rest because the authorities
stopped caring about it."

"I didn't know who else to call. I
couldn't remember any other numbers and
I hid this phone before I even met you
so I didn't have any saved. I know we
didn't leave things the best but can you
help me?"

"I'm not in to any old tech anymore
Cled. I became a cyber not long after we
stopped speaking. You know I'll help if
you need some support though." Beth said
kindly.

"If you could help me get around town,
find a few of my old places and gather
some things, that would be great Beth. I

just want to get all my stuff together, maybe make a few tools and then get out of town. Could you do that for me?"

 "Of course I will C." Beth said endearingly. That was a relief for Cled. If Beth hadn't said yes he had no idea what he would have done. After that they worked out a spot Cled could get to that was just out of town to meet and within an hour they were both there. It was actually quite a nice journey there. Cled hadn't been able to walk far while he was imprisoned so he cherished the moments as he made his way to meet Beth.

 Cled didn't have to wait at the spot that they had agreed to meet at for long. Beth came along the road humming as she read the display of a holographic wrist implant not so different from the one Cled had removed from himself. "Hi C. How've you …" She started before noticing Cled's arm, "What happened to your arm?"

 "I hated it. It was controlling me. Stopping me from thinking my own thoughts. I couldn't handle it so I chopped it off." Cled explained calmly. He'd accepted that it was for the best now but Beth looked horrified. "You got that worried about an arm implant? They don't even have a direct interface to the brain." Beth said as she pointed at a small metal device on the side of her head. "I feel better than ever C. I thought the old tech gave us freedom but we were wrong. Embracing being a cyber is the way to true freedom. They've even started doing mind uploads now. We can live forever!"

Cled just shook his head. He knew that he had lost control with the implant, that he hadn't been him. Maybe that had happened to Beth now too. Although she didn't seem that different, she also didn't feel like the person he had known before. "Let's get going." Cled said avoiding talking about being a cyber any further, "Could you get me to some of my old hideouts?" Cled gave Beth a list. "I just want to collect enough to live off and then leave Howlchester."

Beth led Cled through Howlchester to the places he had asked. Some of them had been taken over or converted in to new buildings making Cled's stashes inaccessible. Cled's things had been taken in others but a few still remained. Walking through the streets Cled was surprised at how much Howlchester had changed since last time he had been there. He didn't recognise anything not even the people. They were so covered in implants that many barely looked human anymore. Beth's implants were nothing in comparison.

As they walked Beth said, "You know you could easily get an arm replacement implant. Some people even chop their arms off to get better implants instead of attaching them to their wrists." Maybe Cled could get something like that. Like Big Bill's arm replacement though. No tracking or connection to the corps. Just a replacements arm. "I'll think about it. I don't want any of this new tech stuff though." Cled said.

"I know you were always against this stuff Cled but I thought maybe you would change your mind. Are you so set on not using cyber tech?" Cled nodded with certainty. "I can't go back Beth. I can't be so shut off from the world. It's suffocating. I don't expect you to understand though. When I had my implant I was almost drawn in and if I had been more accepting to begin with I probably would have just accepted it."

With Beth's maps on her implant they navigated the maze that was the streets of Howlchester quicker than Cled ever had with his holomaps. That with the city layout being more confusing than ever. It was a shame the implants were

77

so intrusive because they also had
genuinely useful features. As they went,
Cled noticed there were no guards now
and no one took a second look at him, It
was like people had forgotten about
non-cybers. By the time they were done
Cled had gathered enough tools and
components to make plenty of old tech,
some of his old devices, sparkcoins and
enough food for a week at least.

  When they got to the edge of the city
it was time for Cled and Beth to part
ways. They stopped and just looked at
each other for a while. Beth was as
beautiful as ever even with the
implants. He regretted that they had
lost touch and that their views on the
world had diverged. He thought about
asking her to come with him but decided
against it. Beth also looked like she
was about to ask Cled something but
stopped herself. Instead Cled said,
"Thanks Beth, you've helped me more than
you could know. Take care of yourself."

  She just said, "Goodbye C," and they
parted ways. Cled walked for a long time
just thinking and hoping to find
somewhere that suited him. He thought
about how his captors had been so angry
that he hadn't become a cyber but the
rest of the world didn't seem to care

anymore. He thought about if he and Beth could have worked. He thought about being the only non-cyber left. It had almost been easier when he was imprisoned to care about being non-cyber. There he was being forced to be a cyber but outside he was free to choose and choosing to be a non-cyber seemed like a lonely choice.

After a few days of camping rough Cled was in to the countryside proper. It shocked him how free the world felt outside of Howlchester. This was the furthest out he had been since he was a child. There were so few people, holomaps weren't needed to navigate and everything felt alive peacefully going about it's business. Cled felt a regret that he had missed this for so much of his life. He had spent so long fighting the cybers and hadn't cared to do what he loved. Tech and nature had been two of Cled's great interests. The cybers had corrupted tech and fighting back against that Cled had forgotten about nature.

Soon Cled found a small village. Most of the inhabitants were cybers but there were surprisingly a few non-cybers too. They all seemed to get along and people seemed to pay no attention to if someone

had an implant or not. On the edge of
the village Cled found a small house for
sale. It was worth less than the sparks
he had brought with him, substantially
less. Cled had made a reasonable amount
selling old tech and prices were always
more expensive in the city but Cled had
never realised how much he truly had.
Cled bought the house without a second
thought and was moved in by the end of
the day. The previous owner was very
happy to be paid in cash.

 After unpacking what he had brought
with him, which didn't take long at all
since he had only brought a backpack
full of supplies from his old stashes,
Cled began work on an cybernetic
enhancement for himself. It was hard to
work with only one arm but Cled had
plenty of time, This would be like none
of the new tech implants, it would be a
replacement arm with no other features.
No corp would be able to track him and
Cled would be able to use it as he had
his old arm. It took Cled some weeks to
complete the arm. He would go in to the
village when he took breaks and buy food
or stop in the local pub briefly but he
was never away from his project for
long.

Finally Cled had completed the arm, it worked exactly as he had wanted it too. Cled added one small finishing touch, where he had once had his tattoo he engraved "Life is better this way." Cled tried the arm out and if felt almost as if he had never lost his arm. With all the tech the corps had made it was easy for Cled to steal the good parts. The arm even allowed Cled to feel touch, even Big Bill's arm hadn't been able to do that.

After extensive testing Cled finally allowed himself to embrace his new home. He went out in to the village, met the locals properly, spent time in the pubs and fields. He began to realise he had enough money to live like this for the rest of his life. Cled never had to work again. The village was beautiful and quiet. Cled only heard about places outside of the village in the pub and that information was a slowly trickle. People would comment on how a few months ago a corp had been bought out or how people were using these new implants in Howlchester. This was often met by a uncaring grunt or a dismissive "Not another one."

After initial introductions, the people of the village accepted Cled as one of their own. They never questioned him too much about his past or his arm. There seemed to be some unwritten village code to never talk about implants people had. Some in the village clearly didn't want implants while other had very reserved ones. It all reminded Cled of the Robot Hound, where no one would question each others choices and that allowed them to exist together without too much trouble.

Being closer to nature also filled Cled with an unexpected joy. He could roam to his content and never found any need for a holomap. Cled could remember the ways of the village and the natural world surrounding it with no issue at all. Why had Cled stayed in Howlchester? He had been surrounded by what he hated and for some reason had spent all of his life there. That didn't matter so much now Cled was out though, he just embraced what he had instead of worrying about his past.

In the evenings Cled would tinker with his own tech as a hobby. He never intended to sell any of it, although it seemed no one cared if people sold or used old tech anymore, he just wanted to make gadgets for his house. He had little automation systems for cooking and temperature regulation. They were

nothing too fancy and the corps made far
better ones but they were Cled's.

Epilogue

Over the years, the village slowly began to use more new tech but the people used it in a different way than those in Howlchester. They never forced tech upon people who didn't have it and seemed to see it as a tool instead of letting it rule their lives like the city dwellers had. Cled found that he didn't hate new tech so much when it was used like this but then he remembered his imprisonment, how the only purpose of the tech seemed to be to control the user. How these people seemed to be unaffected by those systems that were inherent in new tech Cled couldn't understand. Maybe these newer devices were less reliant on that or maybe people here were just more resilient to it. Either way Cled would never know, he would never put himself through that fight he had with himself when he was imprisoned again.

Cled continued to develop his own tech when his arm was finished but it was mostly for personal use or the odd favour for his neighbours who didn't see it as old tech but just tech. His whole house had automations and systems to make life easier, auto clothes washing devices and plant waterers were Cled's favorites. That was only how Cled spent half of his time though, the rest he spent out in this place that he had grown to know unlike any in Howlchester. Cled knew the shape of every building and tree within a few miles of his house, he also knew the inhabitants, human or animal. He spoke to them as he made his way through the paths and woods. In the evenings they would all gather in the pub and talk about nothing much. Cled was the happiest he could remember.

 That wasn't to say there weren't problems in the village. People argued and fought, but those fights were understandable and simple. One man had lost his sheep but accused another of steeling it or someone had crashed a farming vehicle in to a wall. It was nothing like the resentment that cybers had to non-cybers when Cled was in Howlchester. Cled was content, he understood when things went wrong and for the most part they did not.

 One thing had sparked his interest recently though, some people had began rejecting their implants. Many who had been given them as children were now removing them as adults, others had

simpily had enough. This seemed to be
happening more in towns and whenever a
report came through about it the people
in the village would dismiss it saying,
"Oh, not another one," or something like
that. Cled did not and kept his ear open
for any news like that. People were
doing as he had, they had finally had
enough of being controlled by the corps.
 Cled had no intention of going and
fighting the corps again. Doing so had
taken its toll on Cled and he doubted he
could resist another forced implant. He
also simply felt too old to fight now.
Yet general sentiment was changing and
Cled liked to think he had played his
part in it. For so long he had worked
against the corps, he had held out. How
many people Cled had influenced he did
not know, but if he had influenced just
a few to keep fighting then maybe they
had kept the torch alight. Now that
torch was spreading a fire that it
appeared the corps would struggle to
extinguish.

Printed in Great Britain
by Amazon

35947685R00049